The Tenth Circle

The Tenth Circle

by
Mempo Giardinelli

translated by
Andrea G. Labinger

LATIN AMERICAN LITERARY REVIEW PRESS
SERIES: DISCOVERIES
2001

Spanish original: *El décimo infierno*
Editorial Colibrí, Mexico, May 1999.
Editorial Planeta, Argentina, July 1999.

Translation Copyright © 2001 Latin American Literary Review Press

Library of Congress Cataloging-in-Publication Data
Giardinelli, Mempo 1947-
   [Décimo infierno. English]
   The Tenth Circle / by Mempo Giardinelli; translated by Andrea G. Labinger
     p. cm. -- (Series Discoveries)
   ISBN 1-891270-10-9 (alk. paper)
    I. Labinger, Andrea G.

PQ7798.17I277 D4313 2001
863.64--dc21

                                  00-056325

The paper used in this publication meets the minimum requirements of the American National Standard for Permanence of Paper for Printed Library Materials Z39.48-1984∞

Cover Design by David Wallace

Latin American Literary Review Press
121 Edgewood Avenue
Pittsburgh, PA 15218

You are father of fire, kin of flame;
Whosoever most loves you, the more is he consumed;
Love, he who follows you, you burn him body and soul,
You destroy him entirely, like a blaze to a branch.

Arcipreste de Hita, *The Book of Good Love*

My God, brother, to what lengths will we not go
to flee from solitude! What hell would we not visit
to banish our fear!

Jose Manuel Fajardo, *Letter from the End of the World*

For Luis Sepúlveda
And for Osvaldo Soriano, *in memoriam.*

one

I always knew that what I was doing was horrible, but I did it. Once I had launched myself over that ridge of hell, like a bowling ball picking up speed as it slips down the alley, I just couldn't stop. It didn't matter how many pins had to fly. The only thing that mattered was to keep on rolling.

A man who's about to turn fifty and who feels complete in the sense that he's done everything he's ever wanted to do and could, and who finds himself trapped between boredom and restlessness, has only two alternatives: either he begins to prepare for old age, satisfied with what he's done or frustrated by all the things he didn't manage to do; or else he fires off his last round and goes for all-or-nothing. I chose the second option. And Gris put me up to it. Reckless, that's what she is.

I'll tell you something: Resistencia is a town my mother used to call Peyton Place, after a very famous series made during the early years of TV, in black and white. The Devil's Cauldron – I don't know if you remember it. Well, just like Peyton Place, Resistencia is a North American town, only one that ended up in the wrong part of the globe, surrounded by an impressive ring of poverty, like those the North Americans never let anyone see. Nothing ever happens there, until one day, everything happens. The heat drives us crazy, and that's the only explanation for the things that happen, when they happen. I don't understand what triggers it off, but one night – because generally everything occurs at night – we go nuts. You run out of money, or beer, or you get fed up with watching the same old crap on TV, and you feel like you've got to do something. Break something, knock everything down, yell at your neighbor, hit your wife, I don't know, something.

I was burned out, but I wasn't an unhappy man. Before turning fifty, I had already been divorced twice; my kids were in school – one at the University of Buenos Aires and the other one at the National University of Córdoba – and I lived alone in a very big house, the top floor of which had a nice apartment, a sort of enormous loft. On the ground floor, my mother, who was already an old lady, lived with her caretaker, Rosa, a sixtyish woman from Corrientes who was very sweet and efficient. Both of them were very religious and lived simple, peaceful lives, as virtuous as they were boring. I had a good job, independent, with a nice income, that allowed me to be what is smugly known in Resistencia as a good son. My only sin was my secret relationship with Gris. Who was married. Married to my best friend. Don't give me any of that morality crap: everything was

going along great, and for four years it was a perfect relationship. Griselda is a fantastic woman. Not only because she's beautiful, but also because there's no one else in this world you can
have such a good time with: she has a quick, brilliant mind,
and her sharpness is combined with refinement, charm, and
an immense wisdom that both unnerves and fascinates me. And
excuse me, but that's an explosive combination. Passionate and
wild in bed, she was also tired of playing the role of the perfect
middle-class Resistencia lady. By the time we first became lov-
ers, she had already given up going to the Ikebana Club, she
no longer participated in the Cancer Assistance League, and
she had even stopped attending the Holy Trinity School Association meetings. She didn't want to waste any more time in-
venting activities for herself or asking permission or feeling
guilty about anything anymore. What Gris wanted was to have
fun, to enjoy life, to live in the fast lane, and to be loved. All the
things good old Antonio couldn't give her.

We started almost by accident, exactly four years ago,
but I'm not going to tell you how it all began. It's not necessary.
Just believe me when I tell you it was sensational, exciting, and
that never before in my life had I known a woman like that – so
ardent – nor had I ever felt such passion. I had never surren-
dered myself to a woman as I did to her, and I'd never seen a
woman so capable of such total surrender, such emotional com-
pleteness, I mean. We had known each other for a long time, at
least ten years, and I don't think we'd ever had fantasies about
one another. Because of social repression, or whatever it was,
for a decade we had been almost desexualized towards one
another. Until one day – boom! – something exploded, a bomb,
and we entwined like vines beneath rubble, fused together like
two metals in a cauldron.

Griselda was a few years my junior. Seven or eight – I
never knew – because she always lied about her age, and she
did it with absolute, incomparable charm. Lying naked in bed,

she loved when I simply looked at her, slowly masturbating as she writhed around like a contortionist, as sensual as a goddess, while she dared me to exchange her for two twenty-year-olds. Then she would leap on top of me and run her tongue over my body, lingering on the most sensitive parts: my ribs, my armpits, my groin, my ears, and she would order me to hold still, and she possessed me with such elegance, a quality I would be incapable of describing. She mounted me, shifting her hips from side to side, in circles, and she loved it when I caressed her breasts gently; she adored it when I played with her plump nipples, nipples of a mother who has given life, and she closed her eyes and asked me to talk dirty to her, to insult her, to whisper softly that she was the filthiest whore in the whole Chaco. She was fantastic: she was alert to her own pleasure, but also to mine, and as I watched her smile of joy, it was like watching the Mona Lisa before she posed, like imagining the Virgin Mary as she nursed Jesus. And all of a sudden, she would shout at me to give her my milk, to give it all to her, to empty myself out completely in her, and she said she was water, she was the sea, look how she spilled over entirely, and she trembled and ordered me not to hold back, to tell her I loved her while licking her ear, and I did because it was true, because I loved her more than anyone else in the world, and besides, I love talking while I'm doing it, and I knew how it fascinated Griselda that I could make love and talk at the same time.

There's nothing else to say: we loved each other, and after our first meetings, for the first three or four months, when we had gotten over our guilt feelings, we began to tie the most profound bonds of love: the friend she also was, the adviser I also was, the endless talk about our children (her two girls are teenagers already, although they're younger than my kids), the town gossip that amused us so much, our mutual friends and their frustrations, the Nautical Club, the small provincial universe in which we moved. And, of course, we talked about our secret, which was our strength, because from the beginning, we had sworn to speak to no one, absolutely no one, of that relationship. The only thing we never spoke of, the name that was never pronounced, was, of course, Antonio's. Who, in addition to being my friend and her husband, was my partner in Northeastern Argentine Realty, Inc.

Naturally, he knew. At least, I was always convinced he knew. A woman like Griselda can fool an entire town, of course, but not her husband, especially if the husband isn't a fool. And Antonio was no fool. I never understood why he acted like that, but the truth is that he never made the slightest gesture, never asked her questions or showed any anger towards me. Never. He always accepted everything silently. He was a cuckold and he put up with it. That exasperated me and sometimes, enraged, I felt like telling him so, felt like shouting at him not to be such an asshole, that I was stealing his wife; I felt like shaking him and asking him why the hell he put up with it. The truth is I can't say exactly when he found out about us, but I knew that he knew. And Gris also knew that he knew. But we didn't talk about that.

What I'm telling you here is complete idiocy, utter degradation, I know. But I've resolved to tell these things exactly as they were. No holds barred and no pretense. Cards on the table, and all that. When we set that bowling ball in motion down the alley, it was all so explicit and clear that I still laugh at people's innocence. It doesn't even strike me as pathetic; it seems stupid to me. Because people here tend to believe what they shouldn't, and they swallow whatever bullshit they're fed. Urban stupidity is too widespread, too generalized, to let you feel sorry for them. That's a job for politicians or priests, those who always lie and promise things they don't know anything about. So, the most convenient thing to do, at least here, is to be obvious. Subtlety is too much for certain towns to handle.

You can't feed caviar to chickens.

It happened that one afternoon, after making love and ending up as exhausted as if we'd completed the Tour de France, we were smoking a cigarette, and I said to her offhandedly, almost in jest:

"We ought to kill your husband."

And Griselda, without noticing the enormity of my words, as if the important thing was that I hadn't pronounced my friend's name, and without stopping to reproach me at all, not even surprised, simply said:

"And how would we do it?"

two

"I don't know," I replied. "I'll split his head open with a shovel."

She laughed as if I had made a nice, delicate joke, not the kind that deserves a belly laugh, but rather a refined, educated, and perhaps slightly nervous little titter.

But that's just how I did it. It was in their living room the following night. And it was that night for the simple reason that a few hours earlier, in the afternoon, we had collected on three sales contracts that came to nearly two hundred thousand dollars, which we had placed in the company safe and were going to deposit in Banco Río the next morning.

When we had finished eating, like so many other nights when I had gone to their house for dinner and stayed until midnight talking about business, planning one of those commercial transactions that had brought us so many benefits, Antonio and I hung around chatting about the upcoming auction of some lots in Villa Paranacito. It was a new development, which of course wouldn't have everything we were going to offer: the electric lighting and water services hadn't even been bid on yet, and neither had the paving; there were still some problems with the inheritance of a very large family, and in short, we would be the only ones who would benefit: five hundred lots located around a tributary of the Paraná River, really beautiful for a couple of months, in the springtime, but an infested swamp during the rest of the year. Antonio, who was a genius at sales, planned for us to advertise it as a regional paradise of the future, a park-like neighborhood with water, sunshine, and pristine nature, Mercosur's best investment, and that son-of-a-bitch laughed because he knew he could sell ice to an Eskimo.

Griselda got up to make coffee, and a minute later, I interrupted Antonio, saying I had forgotten something in the kitchen, and followed her. Of course, Antonio tolerated that sort of thing. He must have known perfectly well that I would go into the kitchen after her, and there we would grope each other, but he never reacted; he never did a thing. He was my friend, and I know quite well he was no dummy: he was sharp, intelligent, with a brilliant business sense. Why the fuck did he keep quiet, then? I don't know, and I never will, but I've already said that stuff drove me crazy because it reminded me of my mother, who was always so stupid, putting up with my old man's cheating on her for her entire life, and beating her, besides. When I was a kid, my sisters and I grew up listening to those beatings and seeing mama all black and blue, injured, but above all, silent. It drove me crazy, that silence. That not saying anything, that docile acceptance. I hate silence; it kills me, it drives me to despair; I don't understand why people keep quiet and take refuge in that kind of mute suffering. I think I can't stand silent people because they really have a sort of secret, powerful weapon. I don't know, quiet people piss me off. I detest stoics, nice, polite people, all those proper motherfuckers. I would've liked for mama to be less resigned and to put up a fight, protest, say something, or split my old man's head open. But no. Mama's impotence killed me, but in time, I came to despise my own, because lots of times I thought of killing my old man. And I think I didn't do it because he died first. Paradoxically, he was saved by a massive heart attack. If his own goddamned heart hadn't killed him, I would have.

When I entered the kitchen, Griselda was very nervous, out of sorts. I had already told her over the phone that this was the night, and she had overheard the conversation about the money in the safe at the realty company. With a movement of her head, she asked me not to do it, whispering quietly that it was insanity, please, don't, but I went straight for the gardener's shovel that always stood next to the back door of the kitchen. It was made of tempered steel and it still had a bit of dried dirt on the blade. I grabbed it and noticed that Griselda was leaning against the stove, looking at me, simply looking at me with her lovely gray eyes, which suddenly seemed vacant. I hefted the shovel into the air and went back into the dining room and slammed it down with all my might on the back of Antonio's neck.

Just like that, I split his head open with a shovel.

Or that's what I thought at first, because Antonio fell to the floor, collapsing like a duck full of buckshot, but immediately I realized he was still breathing. Although blood had begun to ooze out of his nose and his mouth, a dark little trickle that looked sticky and unpleasant, Antonio was breathing.

I don't know if you've ever killed someone. It's not easy. Or maybe what happens is that life is a stronger impulse than what we normally think. Or maybe there are lives that are incredibly fragile. You've probably heard of those deaths we call senseless: a kid who's riding his bicycle, falls down and dies from a gentle, stupid blow; or the one person who dies in an auto accident because his door opens up while all the others come away unhurt. In any case, those fragile lives exist, lives like butterflies, like insects you squash with a not-so-strong pressure of your hand. But there are other lives that are very hard, that seem like steel, hearts that won't stop beating even when you jump up and down on top of them with Ghurka boots. Well, that son-of-a-bitch Antonio was one of the hard ones. And he kept quiet, naturally, even when he was being killed, he kept quiet, but he was tough, he took it.

When I realized he was still alive, for a second I thought Griselda was going to become hysterical. I raised my eyes to calm her down, but my gaze met her cold, gray eyes, that watched the scene, bedazzled.

"My God, he's alive," she said a few times.

"Bring me a knife, the biggest one you've got in the kitchen."

She went to look for it, and I stayed there, watching that broken body. He must be brain dead, I thought, but it was a healthy body, and that's why it was breathing. I tried to imagine where I'd plunge the knife into him. I didn't want to hit any bones, nor was I interested in butchering him and ending up all stained with blood. Blood disgusts me; I felt revulsion and urgency. I decided to slit his throat.

Griselda tapped me on the shoulder and handed me an enormous Brazilian knife, a gigantic Tramontina I didn't remember ever having seen before in that kitchen. It was perfect.

So I practiced my aim, lowering and then raising the

knife a couple of times above Antonio's throat, and without thinking about it, on the third or fourth try, I discharged it violently, blade down.

It was horrible: the guy gave a jump, as if all the reflex actions of his life had been stored up for that finale; and even though I destroyed his throat and opened up a gash from end to end, nearly separating his head from his torso, he didn't die right away.

I don't understand how he kept on breathing, the son-of-a-bitch, but he was alive. And there was blood everywhere; I even felt it on my cheeks, and it was a warm and thick, like the shaving cream at the barber shop.

I stood up and watched him slowly dying. He was bleeding all over the carpet; his head was tilted to one side like a broken statue, in an impossible, absurd position.

"Impressive," Griselda said.

We looked at each other, astonished, as if we were peeking at the Spectacle of the World for the first time. Her mouth was wide open, and she was breathing agitatedly, just like when she was very excited and turned on.

"And now what do we do?"

"Catch a train," I muttered. "I guess we'll have to run away."

"Please make sure he's dead," she groaned. "Please…"

"He is," I said. "As dead as the last chicken you ate. But now let's get out of here, because the shit's about to hit the fan."

"All right," she said, composing herself and in her normal voice, as if everything had suddenly changed. "Go clean yourself up. I'll be right there."

I obeyed meekly and stood up. My right arm ached, evidently strained by the two huge blows it had discharged. I headed for the back hallway, toward the master bedroom. I planned to take a shower, and I told myself I'd unavoidably have to put on the dead man's clothes. It wouldn't be the first time: we were the same size, and countless times we had exchanged shirts, jackets, and sweaters.

I was about to enter the bedroom when I heard the front doorbell ring.

I froze in my tracks.

three

From the living room, Griselda motioned at me to keep quiet while she went to open the door. It surprised me that she didn't even ask who it was, and by the time I whispered to her to ask before opening it, she was already standing face to face with a fat woman in a bathrobe and a head full of curlers wrapped in a scarf. It was Carmencita Barrios, the wife of one of the most beloved dentists in Resistencia, a very popular guy who had been a Peronist congressman, but not a crook. A very unusual case.

I listened to her saying she'd heard a strange noise and how she didn't want to be nosy, but if Griselda needed anything, well, you know, but if not, she'd better go because it was pretty late already. And while she was saying all this, she didn't stop nodding, as though she were trying to see behind Griselda's back, and of course, she did see. The stupid cow saw me peeking out of the Antonuttis' bedroom, and she must have been impressed by the bloodstains on my shirt because she said:

"Oh, Mr. Romero, are you hurt?"

And with those words, the stupid cow signed her own death sentence.

Griselda didn't block her way; she let her go by. The scene that the woman saw on the dining room floor evidently was too much for her: at first, without understanding, she began to laugh absurdly, thinking maybe it was some kind of joke, nervous laughter, haha, as though the Antonuttis and their friends like to play murder games and stain their clothes and carpets with tomato juice, haha, but right away she caught on that it wasn't a joke, and she stood frozen with her mouth open, wide open, like she was about to prepare a scream, her jaw hanging down over her enormous double chin and gathering air in to let it out again.

Griselda figured it out just as I did and decided that the woman couldn't be allowed to live. Or maybe nothing mattered to her anymore, because she grabbed the poker from the fireplace, that ridiculous fireplace that I made fun of for years because I couldn't stand Antonio's fondness for kitsch, imagine having a fireplace in the Chaco. Griselda gripped the poker firmly and charged at the fat lady like a Roman soldier, shoving it in between her shoulder blades. Just like that, with a single thrust, she stuck it in like a knife into a loaf of bread. I had never seen anything like it; it had never occurred to me that a stick, no matter how thick, could pass through a human back so easily. And I also saw that Griselda's strength was tremendous and her capacity for killing was a brutal as my own.

"Bravo, partner," was all I could get out, with a voice that didn't seem like mine, as though someone else were speaking.

"We'll have to finish her off," Griselda said, and as the woman was squirming on the floor, face down and bleeding like a pig in a slaughterhouse when they cut its jugular after the mortal blow, she took the Brazilian knife I had used to slit Antonio's throat and did the same thing to the fat lady, slicing through the back of her neck like a scythe, and leaving her suddenly as calm and relaxed as an inflatable plastic doll.

"This is crazy," she said. "I can't believe it…"

"We were made for each other, darling," I replied. "All we need now is a quick fuck while we watch the bodies," and I said it laughing nervously, with the same strange, alien voice that was coming out of my mouth but which I couldn't quite recognize.

I can't quite describe how she looked at me: it wasn't exactly suggestive, but she shot me an intense glance with her beautiful, damp, gray eyes.

"Not a chance," I said. "We've got to split before the whole neighborhood collapses."

And so we decided to get out of that house without delay, both of us covered with blood, not caring too much if anyone saw us. Griselda asked me to wait for her for a minute, and she went into the bedroom, where she packed a suitcase with clothes, took all the available money out of the safe, and came back to the living room in a few minutes, during which time I devoted myself to regarding the scene like a cold, businesslike stage manager at the Teatro Colón. She placed a revolver in my hands and bent down to dig around in her husband's wallet.

"We may need it. I hope you know how to use it," she said as she counted the money and put it in her purse. "I found about two thousand bucks altogether. Do you know how to shoot, or don't you?"

"I haven't shot anything since I was in the army, but I can tell when a weapon is loaded or not. And this one's got a full chamber and a silencer, besides."

"I think it's a Colt .38," she said. "One of Antonio's dumb ideas. I never understood why the hell he bought it, but how ironic, huh?"

"What's ironic?".

"That you're the one who's going to use it, you, who knocked him off with a shovel." And she laughed again, a dry, unpleasant laugh that I hadn't ever noticed in her until that night. "Well, okay, let's go."

And at that moment, as we were heading for the door, the bell rang again, and I froze in my tracks once more like a movie freeze-frame, and I couldn't help bursting out laughing. I let out a plain guffaw, as funny as anything.

"It's crazy, I told you," Griselda remarked, and she laughed too.

This time I went to open the door, and I did it just as I was, smiling with all my teeth, with my shirt all full of blood and the jacket in my hand and the .38 under the jacket.

Outside stood one of the kids from Caturro's Pizzeria. He had parked his motorcycle next to the entryway and was looking for an address, a different address.

"Is this…?" he managed to say before he froze, too, seeing me all bloody and seeing God knows what else behind me and Griselda.

"What a shame, kid," I said to him, feeling really sorry and regretting that pointless death, perhaps the stupidest, most pointless death in the world.

And I squeezed the trigger and fired a bullet that hit him in the middle of the chest. The kid looked at me, at first with surprise, with a ridiculous, incredulous smile, and immediately took a step backwards, a very strange thing, as if the bullet had a delayed effect. He spun around like at wind-up toy whose cord is suddenly unleashed, and fell on his back, lying there with his eyes open, as if they were looking for an impossible explanation in the darkness of the sky.

"Let's bring him inside; no one heard anything," Griselda said, bending down and grabbing the boy by one leg to drag him towards the house.

Just then I realized that the shot hadn't produced any noise.

We brought the kid inside the house, and without any clear understanding of what we were doing, almost mechanically, I grabbed the motorcycle and brought it in, too, passing over the boy's body and dropping it in the hallway that led to the living room. Griselda turned off the lights, and as she locked the door, I got into my car and turned the motor on. When she caught up with me, she informed me that she had also brought along some jewelry and her passport, just in case.

As far as I was concerned, at that moment, nothing really mattered at all. The sensation I felt was one of unmatchable excitement, as if my adrenaline had climbed off the charts and couldn't go back down again. I forgot to mention that I've had high blood pressure ever since I was forty, and on occasions like this, the pressure shoots so high that my head hurts a lot, I feel dizzy, with unbearable buzzing in my ears, and, curiously, I get a hard-on. I don't know – it's funny because I don't feel at all well under those circumstances, but it gets hard and stays as hard as a baseball bat. Once I read that this is called something like "priapism" and it's usually very painful. Well, it doesn't hurt me. Or maybe it's because I'm only thinking about my high blood pressure and my fear, that sort of fatal vertigo produced by hypertension.

Well, I didn't care about anything at all at that moment. That's why I hadn't stopped to cover our tracks or do all those stupid things killers do in movies and which seem so precise that a single, tiny little mistake can end up giving them away. No, I didn't give a shit about any of that. And I even liked the fact that no one would have any doubt about who had started that Roman circus.

At any rate, inexplicably, Gris had also brought the knife and the poker into the car.

"Let them struggle a little," she said, laughing. "At least let them have to make an effort to think for a while and tie up loose ends."

"Maybe it'll be too much of a challenge for those pigs," I said, continuing the joke.

And I drove calmly, at normal speed, toward my house.

It was brutally hot, as I've told you, but the two of us preferred to ride with the windows open despite the air conditioning in the car, which I had turned on full blast. There were people on the sidewalk in front of a few bars and cafés, as usual, but we didn't care if they saw us together, at night, and in my car. It was the first, maybe the last, opportunity that town would have to see us together. We had never exposed ourselves; Griselda and I knew, we really knew, that not a single rumor had been spread about us. One of our triumphs, the one we savored most, was precisely the fact that we had managed to throw everyone off track.

So now I allowed myself the pleasure of driving slowly past Clark's, past La Biela, past Nino's, and past all the bars on my way. Let them see us together. Griselda Antonutti with Alfredo Romero. Together, in his car, around midnight on a Tuesday. Let them talk, let them bite their tongues, and let them poison themselves.

four

    I parked by my front door, asked Gris to wait for me in the car, and went inside.

    Let me tell you something about my house because it's my pride and joy. It's one of those big, old-fashioned places known as "sausage houses." I bought it several years ago for a song when the Swedish owners, the Lundgrens, and all their children had died off, and the last remaining daughter, María Luisita the spinster, decided to move to Córdoba. The tough years, when everything was infested with government soldiers and rebels playing war, were over – anyway, we all know what happened even though these days lots of people try to invent a different version of the story – and for me, things hadn't turned out too badly. It was about the time when I separated from my second wife, Cristina, and moved to Misiones Province. I wanted to be as far away as possible from the shithole this country had become, and Posadas turned out to be a pretty calm city where it was possible to be successful. I stayed there for seven years and started in the real estate business. And after Antonio stopped by to visit me on his way to Iguazú Falls with Griselda and the girls, who were still small, we decided to become partners. We still have a branch up there.

Of course, among the first good deals we negotiated was the purchase of his house and mine. So when María Luisita asked us to take care of selling the old Lundgren Mansion, I immediately spied my opportunity. I advised her to ask the market price, but I told her that the market was falling at the moment and that the future of real estate was gloomy; in any case, if she liked, I could buy her out in cash, with seventy percent down immediately, with which sum she could calmly move out, and then I would figure out what to do, assuming the risk myself. She thought it sounded just fine, and since our business had been going incredibly well for the past few years, I had the necessary cash. I worked out the contract to suit my purposes, as it's always possible to do with deaf old Reimúndez, the attorney who owns half of Resistencia and who, more than just an attorney, could and should be considered the shrewdest guy in all the Chaco and environs. In short, I had made the right deal at the right moment.

Well, it's a lovely turn of the century house, which I restored almost completely, installing air conditioning and all the comforts, as they say, with a big Jacuzzi out on the patio next to the barbecue and a long terrace upstairs, where I built the enormous loft that serves at once as my bedroom, private study, living room, and TV room. As I told you, on the ground floor I made all the necessary adaptations so my old lady could live cozily, in a big, modern, comfortable house with a fantastic kitchen and a huge, split-level living room, a place she had always dreamed about but never had before in her entire life.

Yes, I'm very proud of my house, and it doesn't bother me if people notice.

Well, when I walked in, I kissed mama hello. She was very surprised to see my shirt all covered with blood. I reassured her, telling her it was nothing serious, that I'd fallen down on the sidewalk and the stains were no big deal, nothing important. Then we had our typical, innocent, sweet little nightly chat. A very quick report on what we had done that day and how she was feeling, followed by a brief, loving inquiry about how I was and how the business was going, trivial things, but absolutely fundamental to her. Sometimes she even asked me about Antoñito, as she called Griselda's husband, and about Gris herself, of course. Such a lovely couple, she would say, and those two adorable girls, a model family. As I went upstairs to my quarters, she kept bombarding me with advice about my supposed fall, begging me to promise her I'd see the doctor the very next day.

Upstairs, I quickly searched for the couple of thousand dollars I always keep stuck inside my old illustrated Larousse dictionary. I also looked in a pair of pants and another jacket, and in an old wallet where I always used to sock away a few pesos just in case. I gathered all the available cash together, stuffing it into an envelope on which I wrote the words "Cash for Mama" and placed it on my night table.

Then I tossed all my documents, my dark glasses and three checkbooks on my bed, although it was unlikely I'd be able to go to the bank the next day. Maybe I ought to have withdrawn money on all my credit cards, but I didn't want to give myself too many false hopes. As soon as all the shit was discovered, no bank official would cough up a red cent for me, and no one would cash my checks. I took my passport, too, just in case, and I decided that the best thing would be to withdraw as much money as possible that very night from several automatic tellers.

Next I went into the bathroom, took a fast shower, shaved quickly and almost dry, and put on some clean clothes. I gathered up my bloody clothing, making up a bundle to take with me. But then I had a moment of doubt, wondering whether or not to take it along. It was an ethical issue concerning the only thing in the world that mattered to me: my mother. If I took the telltale clothing away with me, she would always have doubts about my part in the killings; on the other hand, if I left everything behind, there would be no doubt whatsoever: the evidence would be incontrovertible. Suddenly, that seemed like the best thing to do for her sake. Certainty may hurt her, I told myself, but doubt would kill her.

So I left everything in the dirty clothes basket, as I did every night. I packed one of those sport bags with a set of underwear, a pair of pants, three shirts, and some loafers. Just in case. I also put in my cell phone with an extra battery, completely charged, and the charger.

When I arrived downstairs, she was still watching TV, while Rosa had one eye on her knitting (let's say a bed jacket in the unlikely event of winter), and the other on God-knows-what show.

"Hey, ma, if they tell you I was the one who started all this shit, believe them. It was me, okay?"

"What are you talking about?"

"Nothing, ma, just some stupid crap, but pay attention and remember: it was really me."

Gris was waiting for me, calmly smoking, for once without worrying about whether anyone would see us, or see her, in a situation that was – well, let's not call it adulterous any more, or even slightly suspicious. Remember: Resistencia is a city where everything people do is always interpreted sinfully, especially if it concerns what a married woman does. Even the official, historical name of the city is San Fernando de la Resistencia, alluding to the border wars with the Indians that for years prevented the establishment of settlements. The present-day city wasn't even founded until the end of the nineteenth century, and apparently the saint lost some prestige, perhaps for moral reasons. I've told you already: Resistencia is Peyton Place, the Devil's Cauldron. A small North American city plunked down by mistake in northeastern Argentina.

First we went to the real estate office where we put all the money from the safe in my briefcase. Before closing it up, I thought that it looked exactly like in the movies: a Samsonsite-type briefcase wide open with both compartments stuffed with bundles of hundred-dollar bills. A thing of beauty: a picture worthy of Pérez Celis, an authentic Kuitca. I walked out laughing, and then we went to Plaza 25 de Mayo.

I drove all around once before parking next to Banco Río, where I withdrew the maximum the ATM would give me: a thousand pesos. I crossed the street and did the same thing at Boston Bank, and then at Lavoro, and finally at Nación. At each one I took out as much as I could, not only with my debit cards but with my credit cards as well. It was a kind of self-purging. I don't know if you've ever tried it, but believe me, it's quite exciting. When it was all over, I had collected a few thousand additional pesos. I had money to spare in those days; I had a good credit rating in the city; and I could write an overdraft at any bank of my choosing.

When I returned to the car, Griselda seemed a bit nervous.

"Are you planning to leave me alone all night?"

"I don't know, but we're gonna need bread for sure. When you've got money, you always know what to do and where to go. So stop bugging me."

I floored the gas violently, because I suddenly felt a little annoyed, and I almost hit a red car that happened to be passing me at that moment. It was one of those sporty Mazdas, an imitation, Asian version of a Ferrari, one of those jobs that the nouveaux-riches, and especially the nouveaux-riches' kids, love so much. Driving this one was a blond, snotty-looking kid accompanied by a young girl with the face of an anorexic. The jerk yelled out a really offensive curse word at me. How can I explain it: under any other circumstances, I swear I would have let the whole episode go, but that night was really very special. I found the insult intolerable and I told him to go fuck himself. Very clearly, enunciating every letter.

And the guy made the mistake of braking his red shitwagon in a very ostentatious way, like he was trying to show off for the anorexic chick so she'd see he was a real macho, the biggest macho in all of Resistencia.

He came towards me, puffing up his chest and cursing me, and he stuck his hand forward to open my car door and pull me out.

I didn't even need to show him the .38. Before he realized it, I had blown one of his eyes out, and the impact made this guy, too, spin on his heels. He fell over like a top that had stopped turning.

I pulled away slowly, passing the Mazda. I looked at the chick inside, bouncing her head like an automaton to the beat of an Argentine rock group that was singing (if you want to call it that) in English. I flashed her a charming smile.

five

Griselda watched me the whole time as if she were evaluating that new man I had become, that different guy sitting next to her. There was astonishment, a slight touch of amazement, quite a bit of curiosity and even amusement in her expression. I was the worst kind of dude: the ideal accomplice for the bad girl she had become at that moment.

You're probably wondering why we did it, what we were looking for. I swear I don't know. The simple truth is I don't know why we did all that stuff. We just kept on rolling and rolling.

We did it, and it fascinated us. Death is like that, now I know. The problem is getting started. And it's not as though I didn't know what I was doing – come on, I knew perfectly well what I was doing; I was fully aware of every one of my actions. No, it was something else: something like dizziness, a kind of hallucination or fascination with my own behavior. I saw the actions I myself was capable of doing passing by at full speed. It was like watching a movie in double-time, like the old Charlie Chaplin films that have fewer frames per second, so they create the illusion of greater speed.

As I thought about all that, and without consulting Griselda, I headed for Route 11, the road to Santa Fe. Gris asked me if we were going to El Monito by any chance. Yes, I replied. El Monito is one of the more traditional motels on the outskirts of Resistencia. Together with the Cadena de Oro and the Okay Motel, it's received the semen and heard the gratified moans of several generations of Resistencia couples. We had gone there a few times, of course, although logically and for obvious reasons of discretion, we preferred to meet in an apartment I had rented right downtown on Avenida Alberdi. It's in an enormous structure containing offices and residences, with almost a hundred condominiums. I used to go there all the time to take a siesta or to watch TV quietly by myself. Griselda had a key, and we had developed a routine: whenever we agreed to spend some time together, she would arrive a half hour before or after me, and she never rode up to my floor, the eighth, but rather she would get off one floor above or below, as if to fool any doorman who might be watching to see where the elevator stopped, and then she'd take the stairs.

But from time to time, she enjoyed going to motels on the route, because, among other things, it amused her to watch herself, to watch us, reflected in the mirrors as we made love. It fascinated her to observe the position of our bodies, and it really knocked her out to see the spectacle of her own orgasms reflected in those mirrors.

I requested a room for the entire night, one of those that were farthest from the road. As we entered, we could still hear the far-off music of Peña Don Atahualpa. Just as we got out of the car, the chords of a classic *chamamé* [1], "Puerto Tirol", were playing, and I also thought I heard a long, triumphant *sapukay* [2].

"Why did we come here?" Griselda asked at that point. "Wouldn't it be better to gain some distance first, to leave the province? Or do you think they won't find us? They might be looking for us right now."

"I don't know. I still haven't thought about it."

And as soon as I closed the door, I grabbed her by the arm and I kissed her and I squeezed her ass in both hands, the way she liked. Gris had – has – one of the most beautiful asses in the world: high and erect, like a teenage gymnast, an incredible thing. Her back rises from it, perfectly formed, ending in a neck and shoulders that are so lovely they look evil. When I grab her like that, like you'd grab a case of first-class wines, and I start kissing her shoulders and feeling her round breasts against my chest, we always end up tumbling into bed, or else I mount her on top of a table, or standing, but it's always me inside her. And often we find ourselves struggling like a bull and a cow, pushing against each other like tractors, but with a muffler, because we have to hold back our screams.

This time, though, we ended up fucking like never before: with unprecedented gentleness, in a exasperatingly slow rhythm, allowing all our inner sounds to come to the surface, she with a constant little cry, like a strange, joyful lament, and I

---

[1] *chamamé*: regional folkloric music of Northeast Argentina, based on polkas and other European musical forms brought to Argentina by the Jesuits in the 16th and 17th centuries. Lively and spirited, it is typically accompanied by concertinas and guitars.

[2] *sapukay*: a Guaraní word, signifying a sharp, loud cry uttered by lumberjacks of the region when felling trees. Also used by indigenous people of the area as a war cry.

with an initial, intermittent vowel, spasmodic and hoarse. That's how we did it, and I don't know how long it lasted, but it was really wonderful. I felt there was nothing else in the world that could make me happier than being inside that woman, feeling like I belonged to her, belonged to her completely as I had never before belonged to anyone. I ended up crying, and that was a very strange thing because she was smiling with her eyes closed and saying it's glorious, this is glorious, what pleasure, what pleasure, and finally we came at the same time. We were lying there, exhausted, and suddenly I started to laugh and she followed me. We must have looked like two lunatics, laughing out loud like *teru-teru* birds, until suddenly and without knowing why, although I tried to restrain myself, I asked her if she felt guilty at all, and she grew serious, very serious, and replied without even thinking about it for a second:

"Guilty of what?"

"Nothing, nothing,…" I said quickly, feeling like what I was: a perfect idiot. "It was a stupid question, don't mind me. The truth is, nothing matters anymore…"

"That's right: nothing matters," she emphasized. "To me, nothing matters at all anymore."

And she lit another cigarette and ducked into the bathroom. I closed my eyes and realized that I wasn't really thinking about anything: in a few more seconds, I would fall asleep, just as I always fall asleep after making love. My mind was a blank. It was simply a question of relaxing my muscles. I fell asleep, mentally repeating several times, "Nothing matters to me anymore, nothing matters any more."

But of course I still didn't understand just how true those words were.

six

Griselda woke me after a couple of hours. It was almost two-thirty in the morning, and the heat was still stifling and intense. Not even the air conditioning in the room could alleviate the effects of that fiery night.

"You've had a nice rest," she said, placing a lighted cigarette in my mouth. "Now we've got to keep going."

"Going? Where? How?" I took a long drag on the butt.

"Questions for a philosopher," she said. "Who are we? Where do we come from? Where are we going? You forgot to add when and why."

"Or maybe questions for a witch."

"I'm your python-woman" she said, laughing and making an adorable face. "Never forget it: your sorceress is named Griselda."

I took a quick shower while she, having showered earlier, finished getting dressed. She put on a yellow, floral-print dress, with a short, flared skirt and a very low neckline. She adored that dress, not only because I had bought it for her in the States but also because it accomplished several things: it looked fantastic on her; it was cool and comfortable; and it really showed off her perfect legs and her magnificent tits.

"Mmmmm…" I commented, emerging from the bathroom and watching her admire herself in the mirror. "Madam, you're going to give me a heart attack."

"After tonight, nothing will ever give you a heart attack," she said, opening the door and standing in the illuminated doorway, as though she were swallowing the first mouthful of that thick, hot air coming from the mountain.

I was surprised to see her standing there with the door open. Until that night, whenever we had gone to hotels, we took great pains so that no one would see her: before entering the hotel room, and later, before leaving, I always turned off the lights, peeked out, scrutinized the darkness to make sure no one was watching our bungalow, and then I would open the car door, keeping the overhead light off so she could climb in quickly, nearly always covering her head with one of my sport coats, a jacket, or whatever.

As we got into the car, I pointed out my observation: although it was obvious that she no longer cared if people saw her, I told her I seemed to notice a certain defiance in her.

"Who am I defying?" she said dryly, almost unpleasantly. "The mosquitoes and the other bugs? This shitty town?"

I kept quiet. I knew she needed my silence: that way,

she would consider her speech finished, or else she'd start talking to herself, of her own accord. I waited, smoking as I drove along slowly. She chose the second option.

"Suddenly I realized how much I've been pretending, you know? My whole life long, I mean, not just since I've been with you...I've spent my life faking it, forced to make a good impression on other people, never doing what I wanted just for the pure joy of doing it. I was repressed by my folks, the nuns at Holy Trinity, my husband, my kids, society, the whole fucking world...Forty-two years making sure everything was just so all around me, taking care of a family, a house, a job...I spent my life trying to make everybody else happy...stupid me, the idiot who never had the slightest idea of what happiness was."

She hurled her cigarette butt out into the night, with obvious anger, just like an annoyed truck driver. And immediately she pushed in the car cigarette lighter and lit up again. She blew out the smoke forcefully.

"Once, a nun I loved very much and who was my friend, Sister Herminia, a sweet, young woman, confessed to me that she didn't know what happiness was, either, and that's why she had married God. 'At least it gives me some peace,' she said, and ever since then I've always wondered why the hell I didn't feel the same way. For years I felt guilty because I thought my faith was too small, a weak, defective faith...Later, when I married Antonio, I realized he was the best man I'd ever have, and I swore to be faithful to him and care for him and be a good wife. And I think I was. I was a good mother, too – I am. I never failed to provide the people around me with support, understanding, love. I can even say I spent my whole life giving things up...But now my girls are in Rosario, and I know they're all right. And my folks aren't around any more; I took care of them till the end, like a good daughter. I still visit my sister in San Luis every summer, or else she comes here with her family. I never refused to go anywhere with Antonio; I followed him wherever he wanted to go. I always did the right thing. There, you see? I joined committees, I went to Mass, I helped out with the PTA, I'm a member of the board of the Holy Trinity School, I make donations to the Barefoot Carmelites. I was always a model wife to my husband, an ideal mother to my daughters, a perfect daughter to my parents, a flawless lady according to the little provincial society I live in, someone who never allowed herself any transgressions except one or two small lapses like arriving home a half hour late, apologizing…One whose only, secret sin began when you appeared. The first time, I don't know, now I think I must have been a fertile field. Not to minimize any of your charm, understand, but I had reached my melting point…If it hadn't been you, it would have been someone else, Alfredo. Of course, I'm glad it was you. I love you. I loved you right away. You knew how to be my man, to be essential to me in the most intimate ways. You fucked me like no one else; you taught me to enjoy doing it like a bitch, like a sow, I don't know, whichever female animal loves doing it the most. And most of all, without even intending to, you showed me another path: the path of sin, but not just for sin's sake. Or maybe it *was* that way, at the beginning, yes, it was a kind of bedazzlement, you know…I prematurely fulfilled all the obligations life, or other people, imposed on me. But I'm still young, and now I want other things. It's time for me to think of myself and my desires, and I feel beautiful, desirable, and I want to have fun, and I want to do a million things I never did, because I didn't dare, because I stopped myself or else I was stopped. I'm fed up with prohibitions, with cancellations, with asking permission, with being proper…All of that still hurts me; it's unbearable. That's why, after the initial bedazzlement, I started to realize everything was much more profound…And I understood that the other path was simply that: another path, something else, something different – that a woman can desire, that she has the right to desire and get things, because they're things that a woman like me, so repressed and proper, has always wanted and will always want. Always, you understand?"

I had the impression she was crying. Just in case, and since I had no idea where I was going, I drove slowly. I got on the road to the airport, just to circle around without driving into the city. For a moment I thought the police might already be after us. I also asked myself how long it would take them to discover the bodies, and if perhaps some relative of that fat Barrios woman mightn't have already gone to see why she was so late.

But I told myself that it didn't matter to me at all. And it was true: at that precise moment, I didn't give a damn about anything that didn't have to do with what Griselda was saying.

She took out a Kleenex, blew her nose, and continued:

"I'm angry, Alfredo...I'm furious. I can't understand why I was always so dumb. I'm resentful, and nothing at all matters to me. Tonight I feel like I could do anything, you know? Besides being a python-woman and a whore, I feel like a harpy, a basilisk..."

"Sorry to interrupt you, Gris," I said abruptly, seeing the lights of a highway patrol car at the intersection of Route 11 and Soberanía. "But look at that."

"I'm looking," she said. "But don't even think about stopping."

seven

The patrol car flashed its lights at us, and even though Griselda protested, I thought it best to stop. I left her in the car and got out. I made up my mind right then and there, when I noticed there were two cops inside. I could take them on perfectly well. In fact, I was eager to – because they were corrupt and inept. I hate the police, and I've always wanted to have a tank or an armored car so I could run down the highway patrol. A kind of impregnable batmobile to flatten cops with. And it's not like I'm one of those anarchists who think you have to destroy all authority, oh no, it's not that. I believe fervently in authority, in hierarchies, and in the premise that it's not true we're all created equal, because we're not. Even better: if it were up to me, there would be a first-rate police force: well-educated cops with university degrees and modern firearms and technology – real knights at the service of the community. But not these bums, this human carrion in uniform, ignorant and full of themselves, trained only to take bribes and use electric cattle prods on the balls of chicken thieves. These pigs make me sick to my stomach.

So I went over to the patrol car slowly, and before they could say anything to me, I told them I was a close friend of the governor and that I worked as a consultant in the Ministry of Public Health, and I'd really appreciate it if they could help me with a problem I had in the trunk of the car. The idiots immediately forgot their reason, whatever it may have been, for making me pull over, consulted each other quickly, and one of them got out and walked towards me. He was a fat guy with a ridiculous, half bow-legged gait, as though he had plantar warts or they had issued him shoes a size too small. Although it was dark out, I thought I noticed that he had a grease stain on his shirt, right on the belly, like he'd spilled tomato sauce or something like that on himself. I felt repulsed, and at the same time, I told myself it was a shame, a real injustice, that some woman in the world had to bear that animal on top of her, even for a single night of her life.

I headed toward the trunk of my car, my back toward him. I opened the trunk, muttering something, any old thing, and ending with the clearly pronounced word "please." I grabbed the tire wrench, pulling it out sideways without the fat guy's noticing it. I asked him to come closer and pointed inside the trunk. The idiot leaned forward to see. I broke his neck with the wrench.

He collapsed to the ground like what he was: a pile of

amorphous fat. I quickly took his pistol, a Ballester Molina .45, which I recognized immediately: it was just like the ones we used to use in the service. I stuck it in my waistband, in back, and grabbed what used to be Antonio's .38. I loved having a revolver with a silencer. It makes a fantastic sound, just a little snap, like a gob of guanaco spit – click, clack – and you blow the shit out of whichever dummy you happen to be facing.

I called out to the other cop, like it was urgent, telling him that his partner had collapsed. This guy, skinnier and shorter (a sort of Laurel and Hardy of the Chaco Police Department), came towards me all worried, asking, what's the matter, what's the matter?

"This is the matter," I said when he was six feet away from me, nailing a bullet right into the middle of his face. Click! and the repulsive asshole went straight to hell. I loved that stuff. Believe me, it's fascinating to go around killing people. Yeah, I know perfectly well that it probably sounds absurd, horrible, but try it for yourselves and tell me what you think.

Griselda got out of the car, looked at the scene, and said, "Hey, you're crazy – you can't stop."

I ordered her to look and see if there was another weapon inside the police car while I took the .45 from the skinny guy, who was spread-eagled on the ground. She did everything very slowly, almost in slow motion, as if she were very tired or she couldn't give less of a damn about what was happening in the world. She returned empty-handed, sat down inside the car again, and straightened her skirt, pulling it over her perfect thighs. I stood there for a few seconds, admiring her legs. They're magnificent, unique. The best legs in the world. I don't know if I told you that Griselda was a ballerina as a girl: she was in the ballet corps at the university and she would have made it to the Teatro Colón if she hadn't been frustrated by I forget what argument from her parents, who wouldn't let her.

I threw it into first, and off we went, burning rubber.

There was a Shell station on the corner. There I asked the kid who was pumping gas to fill it up. We remained silent inside the car. Griselda looked straight ahead, towards the plaza, as though she were engaged in a mute dialogue with something or someone. Her eyes were sort of vacant. Or else too full of a bunch of things I didn't know about, couldn't know about.

I thought, everything is just beginning. Or rather, I realized that some tie had been severed, some thread had slipped out of place. An error had been made, let's say, in the assembly line. And as soon as it happened, everything went into crisis mode, everything turned upside down, the abnormal became normal, and at a dizzying speed, besides. In one second the world itself seemed to have changed. I remembered how once, on a trip through Germany, when I was about to visit the Cologne Cathedral, I had saved myself from taking the Intercity, which later became known as the Death Train. The bullet train had gotten derailed in the middle of the night; the locomotive crashed into the station, and fifteen cars piled up one on top of the other, the so-called accordion effect, and it was a disaster: a heap of dead and dying, and a big, fucking government crisis. I still don't know why I chose to stay an hour longer in the cathedral and didn't take that train, which I had tickets for. But that's the way it is: it takes just one little gear slipping out of place to make everything explode, everything change. People have no idea how fragile life is. And yet almost everyone goes around like an imbecile worrying about what's ephemeral, protecting and saving what's destined to disappear. It's funny, after all.

I laughed to myself as I thought about all this. In less than – how long? – two hours, let's say, I had created a phenomenal mess. And then they tell you in the movies that druggies or drunks do these things, or kids who were misunderstood by their parents: all the moralists who make movies can go fuck themselves. Almost everyone who makes movies is a son-of-a-bitch.

The kid returned my keys to me, I paid him, and he thanked me for the tip I had given him, which was unusually generous. I pulled away, immediately lighting a cigarette, and I drove with concentration, convinced that I, too, was simply discovering evil. I, too, I say. And let no one judge me, please – save yourselves the trouble. No one in this perverse country has the right to judge anyone else, understood? Let no one dare judge me in this country where, after the military, who were incompetent pigs, those in power now are Mafiosi, thieves, and sons-of-bitches. The only difference seems to be that these guys have nicer manners. They're more respectable, sure, and the bankers are happy, not just because they're lining their pockets, but also because the nouveaux-riches learn good manners fast. And I learned good manners, too, of course, but, hey, I was a decent guy: I never shit on anybody; I was a perfect asshole. And then I got fed up – end of story, okay? That's all: Romero was a terrific guy, a decent man, who would've thought?...they can say all that...But it's also good for them to know that Romero got tired of being such a fucking, useless, upright jerk. Nice and clear, just like that, and so no one will judge me: I got fed up, and now they can all suck my dick. So get it straight, guys, don't be shocked, because around here no one can point a finger at anyone else, no one can throw the first stone at me, no one's ass is so clean that he can sniff around in someone else's pants.

So let's not have the moralists judge me, then, those who destroyed a couple of generations in this country. There's no more hope for them. No more. This country has no cure for those guys. Ever since we've been taken over by drug pushers, and people have started to feel nostalgic for the dictators, it's obvious that the only destiny for this society is severity. Weaklings are trampling our values, so don't talk to me about values. What values? Whose? And why do I have to be the one to respect them? And don't give me that crap about the younger generation: I don't think my kids' generation is any better. Not necessarily, and there's no evidence of it. So let's not allow ourselves to be judged by the sweet, innocent souls or the flesh merchants who prostitute little girls, or those who oppose legalizing drugs while dealing themselves, or those sons-of-bitches who can't even cry at the deaths of their own children. Or those who change their identity, or who fake suicide, those who hire assassins, those who sell their souls, those everyday Lucifers, or, in short, those who traffic in other people's lives every day, let them not judge me, goddammit – they ought to invent a tenth circle of hell for all of them, for those guys who pontificate and lie, for the hypocrites and cynics who are debasing this country, for the violent ones who preach peace, for those who bless anyone who pays them and for those who are blessed by any arbitrary charlatan. A tenth circle of hell, too, for cowards, for those who lecture at universities, those who write for a living, those who censor debates and thought, sincere phonies, sinners on TV, addicts of TV, plastic, proper people, those who applaud politely over the table and rub their balls underneath, people who smile at those in power, professional ass-kissers, those who remain bureaucrats forever because they know how to land on their feet, those who always get along and carve a little niche for themselves wherever the grass is greener, those who mutter under their breaths, and the oh-so-nicely mannered. There's no more hope: this is a country of sheep and desperate men.

I don't know if I've made myself clear: I don't give a damn if you think I'm bitter, or a psychopath, or Jesus Christ on roller skates. I don't give a shit about what you think or don't think: what I'm saying is I won't allow anyone to judge me or evaluate everything I did, what we did from the moment this story began, when Gris and I decided to kill her husband. A little respect, ladies and gentlemen, a moment of silence for

49

such an accumulation of tragedies. Just a tad of discretion, all right?

And with these thoughts on my mind, we left the city and I took the bridge to Corrientes. I thought I was heading there simply in order to throw the knife and the poker into the Paraná, from high above, that is, from about three hundred feet up. It would be impossible to find anything thrown into that river from that height, because of its depth at that point and the unusual force of the current. They'd never find the murder weapons, I told myself jokingly. Let them struggle – why make it easy for them? If it were up to me, to us, nothing would be easy for anyone. And it wasn't going to be.

eight

As we were crossing the bridge, Griselda suggested that we continue to Posadas and cross over into Encarnación from there. Later we could head north through Paraguay and enter Brazil through El Pantanal or through Corumbá, and then we'd decide: whether to continue, to disappear into the Matto Grosso, to cross the Amazon and arrive up north, near the Guyanas, through Amapá, and settle down in a cabin by the sea.

She was crazy. I listened to her, wondering if she was delirious or if it simply amused her to imagine such a trek.

"They'll hunt us down like a couple of deer," I told her. "If we move around that much, eventually they'll find us. What we should do is find some place to settle down and lay low there for a while."

"Okay, we'll do whatever you want. After all, nothing matters to me any more – I've told you that already."

"Not even your girls?"

I saw, or rather I felt, her neck tense, and her mouth formed a fierce, perhaps involuntary, grimace.

"They'll be all right, so don't get them involved in this, goddamn it, Alfredo," she said, very coldly. "I don't want to think about them or about anything that ties me to anything anymore, I've told you. So stop screwing around with me. Let it be. Enough."

I shut up and decided to evaluate what she was proposing. I thought it might be necessary to change cars in order to change countries. I quickly figured out that the only car I could take that same night belonged to Asad, the Turk. A friend of Antonio's and Griselda's as well, he kept his car in the garage at the Chaco Medical Association, where he was one of the directors. The night watchmen knew me, and if I showed up with some supposedly urgent message from Doctor Asad, they'd give me the keys without hesitating for an instant. I couldn't help smiling as I imagined the Turk's face the next day: he's a real car nut, and he had just bought a beautiful Land Rover, the most expensive, exclusive model. They'd hear him cursing all the way to the Orinoco.

But I decided it would be better to stay with my own car. Because of the papers, and because we could be crossing the border in three hours, before anyone could figure out anything, or at least before any order for our arrest could reach the Posadas-Encarnación bridge. All the bridges at the border are protected by the National Guard, and the *gendarmes* hate the provincial police because they're just as corrupt, but much more inept, than they are. I smiled again, telling myself that the Turk's Land Rover had been saved by a hair.

"May I ask what's so funny?" Griselda inquired in a disagreeable voice.

"Nothing to share," I responded dryly. "But you'd better improve your mood because we've got a long trip ahead of us."

"Is that a threat, Mr. I-Laugh-Alone?"

"Take it any way you want, but change your mood."

"What if I don't feel like it?"

I don't know what happened to me, don't ask me why, but I hit the brakes violently. She recovered right away, and like a boxer who receives a blow and knows that his life is riding on returning it immediately, giving back two for one, if possible, she threw herself on top of me, insulting me fiercely and clawing me like a cat. I tried to grab her wrists, but only got halfway. During the struggle, she managed to scratch my face, near my right eye. She was unstrung, completely beside herself, so I had no choice but to land a punch right in the middle of her nose.

I've got a very heavy hand, as I've told you, and although I'm not in the habit of fist-fighting – in fact, I repeat, I had never hit anyone before – I know that my hand is very heavy. So I unleashed it in the middle of her face, and I felt something like a little creak under her skin, a soft crack, like something had broken down there. A bone, her nose, a tooth – I don't know – I broke something of hers, and she let out a very soft, deeply pained, "Ow!", like a final sigh, and went to sleep. Groggy. Knockout.

I sat there watching her for a while, noticing a purplish bruise spreading around her nose and under her eyes, which were starting to swell as if she had been crying for two days in a row. I looked at myself in the rear-view mirror, and I saw that a little trickle of blood was running down my cheek next to my right eye. I dabbed it with my handkerchief. Then I seized the steering wheel and stared out at the night beyond the windshield. We were on the slope, just before the Casino, in a very dark area. I was furious. I thought about killing her right then and there: it was three AM – the perfect time and place. But love – or what remained of love – I don't know, whatever you want to call that thing I still felt for Griselda – held me back. There, and at that moment, I realized that rage can really be an uncontainable sin; anger blinds you, leads you astray, and when you see all your paths closed, all you want to do is break down the barriers, hurl yourself against them like a buffalo, punish like you were God. Someone who has killed and can no longer stop himself can cross the line with the power of a bull, that animal brutality that will break down barbed wire fences and stockades without a second thought, and he'll be ready to die in the attempt, but he'll never stop pushing and pushing. Rage is a runaway bull, I told myself, and I was rage itself at that moment.

Only the silence of the night, the slow quieting of my breathing and Griselda's gentle, troubled wheezing as she dozed by my side managed to calm me down. She shifted slightly, and her dress slipped up her leg a bit, and in the tenuous reflection of the headlights, her legs gleamed and I got hot. Her tiny, immaculate white panties were showing, contrasting against the sleek darkness of her skin, smooth as the surface of a lake shining in the sunlight at one in the afternoon. I knew that underneath her dress, there was only Griselda, naked. She rarely wore a bra, proud of her full, broad, plump breasts, a mother's breasts but still firm, high, generous. I adored them, and she adored it when I gently sucked them like a baby who licks the last little drops of dessert as he sweetly falls asleep. As I looked at her, telling myself how lucky I was to have fallen in love with such a woman, I felt something moving in my groin; like a muffled whisper, my organ rose in my pants, demanding freedom to do battle. I opened my fly, and as I took out my member, I leaned all the way over to sink my face into Griselda's crotch. I ran my tongue over the little bit of cloth of her bikini panty, and I began to suck her, gently at first, and then, when she immediately responded as if awakening from a beautiful dream and not a nightmare, with all the force of my mouth: my tongue, transformed into a succession of lizards, rubbed against her clitoris, making her jump electrically, so that she seemed to be levitating, like an epileptic, above the seat.

Then she asked me to penetrate her; she begged me to break her apart, to hit her again, to do whatever I wanted to her because I was an unforgivable, God-forsaken son-of-a-bitch but I was a marvelous son-of-a-bitch who made her love it like no one else in her whole life had ever done.

You'll pardon me, but there's no macho in this world who won't respond accordingly to demands like that. I was rage, and I was a runaway bull, all at the same time, and at that very moment. She had a series of orgasms, and at the end, when I reached my own, I felt her so submissive and so fragile beneath me, I felt her so broken, I mean, that I got up gently and looked at her face again. Her eyes were closed, with a look of pain that was too expressive, too profound, and I ejaculated with a fierce groan, pronouncing her name over and over and over again, thinking I would be capable of doing anything for that woman, really anything, even killing her.

nine

A little bit of blood, maybe a broken tooth. That was all that was wrong with her, really. As I lovingly rubbed my handkerchief, moistened with saliva, over her face, I thought that although what I had done was probably very wrong, it was nothing, after all, compared with so many guys I knew, who surely hadn't killed anybody and who maybe weren't even adulterers and who might even have been very good fathers, but nonetheless were consummate cretins, practically professional evildoers, brutes behind closed doors, blackmailers, and the worst sort of cynics. I knew all about Marcela's – my first wife's – parents, and how they destroyed her life, the old man with beatings, the mother consenting to the violence, both of them partners in the abuse of their children, and about my father-in-law's brother, Marcela's most beloved uncle, who made his niece suck him off when she was seven years old and who even made it with his own daughter, Elisita, when she was only fourteen.

No, that son-of-a-bitch hadn't killed anyone, and he walked around loose in the same city as I did. You could still find him in La Biela, any afternoon or evening, drinking whisky with his buddies until dawn. And my own father-in-law, the grandfather of my kids – he hadn't killed anyone, either, but his daughter hated him thoroughly for his violence and betrayal, because the bastard continued to beat her until she married me: in fact, one day I was the one who threatened him, going against all the principles I then held:

"If you ever touch a hair on Marcela's head again, even if you *are* her father, I'll kill you. Just like that. And don't say I didn't warn you."

I must have seemed convincing then. Or maybe I was just convinced myself, because that man detested me for practically his whole life, but he never dared go near Marcela again, and he respected me more and more. And even when we separated, he told his daughter she was losing an ideal husband.

That's the kind of hypocrisy that kills me in Peyton Place. I can think of so many similar cases – well, we all know of them. For example, old Di Tomasso, who's been fooling around with the wife of Kobalsky the Russian for almost twenty years: in fact, they're a couple who can be found in Buenos Aires or in Rosario. Lost of people have seen them, and yet Di Tomasso is president of the cooperative of Great Works of Sacred Immaculate Heart High School, Jacobo's wife conducts the Municipal Philharmonic Choir, and Kobalsky himself presides over the Regional Economic Federation, and it's a well-known fact that every Friday and Saturday he goes to the whorehouses in Corrientes. None of them had killed anyone, not even a fly, maybe, but they're all a bunch of filthy pigs.

And Chiquita Ferraro, daughter of the most famous physician El Chaco has ever produced: isn't she the mother of a child she had by her own father, a Distinguished Professor at the University medical school?

None of them is an assassin, but they all avoid paying taxes, they all steal public funds, and all of them know the best shortcuts to gracious living. Those who are in politics do it by serving themselves from the collective pot, from the bureaucracy, from the corrupting sinecure system that they themselves created and continue to develop. Those who aren't in politics do it by raising the price of cheap goods, wreaking havoc with the environment, pillaging what might otherwise be conserved, riding roughshod over the city's beauty with their bad taste. They all summer in Santa Catarina or in the Caribbean; they all travel to Miami and sometimes to Europe, and they're all diplomats in their latest-model Mercedes Benzes or BMWs or Hondas, and all at the expense of other people's misery, other people's muck: depraved, perverse types with the calling card of respectability, with pedigrees as phony as a three-dollar bill.

But none of them ever killed anyone. None of them can be accused of assassinating anyone. None of them.

I finished cleaning up Griselda's cheek, and I kissed her on the nose. It was ugly, black and blue. Despite the darkness, you could see a swelling forming on that skin I loved. I felt guilty, horrible; I felt like more of a monster for having hit her than for all the blows and gunshots that had come from my hand that night. Because it was a hideous night – and I was well aware of it. I'm not about to tell you I didn't know what I was doing, okay? Man, did I ever know, I knew it at every moment...I could spend my whole life sighing with regrets, sincere or otherwise, but I won't say I didn't know what I was doing. That's why my guilt was so precise at that moment: that purple bruise on Griselda's face was more accusing, more condemning, than the three or four murders of the past few hours.

Surely, I thought, the difference was in the uncontrollable desire, the mutual passion, the love – sick, if you will, but love, after all – that we had for each other. Also in the dreams we shared, of course. At that moment, I recalled how we managed our guilt at the beginning, the fear she inspired in me at first, and, yes, all the crazy happiness that falling in love produced in me, in love at last with a perfect woman, perfect for me, adorable, magnificent, brilliant – a woman who had it all. Including a husband who was my friend and who obviously was in the way.

In short, we still had a long way to go together, that night and the days that were to follow. The night is long, I said to myself, and tomorrow is always uncertain. And consequently, the question I asked myself as I crossed the city of Corrientes, which slept with the same single-mindedness with which it prays and sings, wasn't when or how, or even why. The question I asked myself had to do with limits. Where were they? Did limits exist? And the answer, obviously, was that there were no limits, there were none anymore, because I was the son, perhaps one of the most sincere sons, of a country in which the only thing that was true and patently clear was that having no limits was the norm, that anything anyone's imagination might invent was possible and that in any case it was a question of finding out how extravagant or wild your own imagination could be.

I got on Route 12, heading toward Posadas. As soon as we had passed the old Cambá Punta Airport, the police stopped us. Just routine: a fat guy, half-asleep, moved his head as if to see if anyone was in the back seat, asked me where we were going, and after I told him we were going to pray to the Virgin of Itatí nice and early, he nodded to me as he said ceremoniously:

"Good evening, sir, and have a nice trip."

With the same degree of ceremoniousness, I crossed myself and pulled away. When the guy could no longer see me, I burst out laughing. Griselda lovingly placed her hand on my thigh.

"You're divine," she said. "The cruelest, most disgusting, most divine son-of-a-bitch."

And she turned on the radio but we could hear only noise, music that sounded like it was coming from an old 78. I told myself that the mystery would be to figure out how long we had to keep running away. I'd find out pretty soon.

ten

I was afraid of falling asleep during the trip, because I was exhausted. My right arm hurt, from the shoulder down to each fingernail, and besides, I felt like my kidneys were swollen, I don't know, like someone had kicked me in both ribs. Pure tension, I told myself, and I also told myself I had no options. Looking in the glove compartment, I found a pillbox with some aspirins. I always carry them. The red ones, the strongest kind. I swallowed three. They tasted so disgusting I felt like vomiting. Then I realized I was hungry, too.

I stopped at an Esso station and asked Griselda to get out and buy me a sandwich, a soda, and some strong coffee. She did, and we ate inside the car, with the door open, at the side of the gas station. I pulled away with the coffee still steaming. Griselda had also restocked our cigarette supply, so we smoked in silence. I calculated that in two-and-a-half hours we'd be crossing the bridge from Posadas to Encarnación. At that hour of the morning, I told myself, the *gendarmes* were unlikely to bother us, and in any case, it was merely a question of having a few dollars in small change. On both sides of the border, if you have an assortment of low-denomination bills, you can get absolutely anything across, in one sense or another. The coin of the realm at the Argentine-Paraguayan border is called Corruption. It speaks many languages: everyone understands it.

Once across, I'd phone Eleuterio. He was a guy Antonio and I had helped a few times in some rather dubious matters, quick documents for land purchased in Formosa and in El Chaco, for astronomical sums, without asking questions and with papers that should have been obviously detectable. He had paid us very well each time, but we had always fulfilled our end of the bargain in such an impeccable way that he sent us cases of the most expensive Scotch every Christmas, and more than once he had emphasized that the day we needed his help, in any shape or form, we needed only to let him know. Well, now that day had arrived.

I felt tired, and also a little frightened, in a way. Or maybe it wasn't that, exactly. Maybe it was the astonishment I caused myself, which I suddenly couldn't interpret. I couldn't quite understand if that guy who was running away was really me, if it was a dream, a nightmare from which I would awaken in a few hours, things you think about in situations like that. You can't imagine the number of strange things one is capable of thinking about in an extreme situation. And I was: I was in mid-flight, and I knew that every minute was beginning to acquire an incalculable value. I had no way of knowing at what moment the bodies in Antonio's house would be discovered, if the neighbors would show up, the people from the pizzeria, the cops, or whoever. Trying to guess made no sense. And I had no way of knowing what that little bitch in the red Mazda might have said, either. Or at what moment the cops would tie up the loose ends of all the crimes, but surely they had already found the patrol car and the fat cop and the skinny one. Maybe they were already on our trail; maybe we still had some time.

What was certain was that by dawn, one way or another, we had to be on the other side of the river, in Paraguayan territory.

Then I jerked in my seat, understanding the cause of my fright: suddenly I realized that getting to Posadas might not be difficult, but crossing over into Encarnación was an illusion. No matter how idiotic and inefficient the Chaco cops might be, they would have already dispatched a pile of border control alerts, at the very least, out of a feeling of *esprit de corps* and because they were furious. They weren't so dumb as not to realize that the first thing a couple like us, who had created such a major fuck-up, would do would be to try to cross into Paraguay.

Suddenly I saw very clearly that they were going to hunt us down like rats, right on that very bridge. I felt my sphincter contracting.

"Gris, I'm beginning to think we might not have enough time to cross over from Posadas…"

"I was thinking exactly the same thing. I'm sorry I gave you the idea of going there."

We remained silent for a few seconds. I saw the entrance to Itatí. There were some lights up ahead there. I slowed down.

"What do you plan to do?"

"We have to cross the river right away, don't we? We can

do it from any one of these towns, and we will."

"And how are we going to get our hands on a boat or someone to take us across? Or are you planning to swim?"

"We'll find something, someone. I don't know…we'll go to the wharf and see. I haven't been to Itatí in years, but I as I recall, there's a wharf."

"Fine," she said, lighting two cigarettes and passing one to me while I took the access road into town. "Let's say, then, that our situation is desperate, so we'll proceed like desperate people. We'll cross from here, no matter what happens."

"That's my girl," I said, and I hit the accelerator at full speed, heading for the town.

eleven

From the highway to the town, it's less than six miles, which we covered in a couple of minutes. I was going very fast, around eighty-five, and I barely slowed down when I saw the gigantic silhouette of the basilica outlined in the night shadows. It's a mass around three hundred feet high, with a cupola that some ecclesiastical architect must have imagined would rival Saint Peter's, or something like that. It turned out to be an enormous thing, a typical mixture of styles and – Argentine, naturally – never finished. But it has an immense capacity: you could probably fit thousands of faithful inside, and every year they hold a couple of pilgrimages that are really impressive for their sheer numbers, one in September, and the other, of course, for the Virgin's Feast Day, which is the chief event in Corrientes and in the entire region.

The town, which probably has around five thousand permanent residents, was sound asleep. It was after four AM. But it was as hot as hell, and as is well know, that's a guarantee some people will be awake. Insomniacs, whores, and desperate people are the night watchmen in all the towns on the planet. And in Itatí there were doubtless all three categories.

A couple of girls were chatting in the enormous plaza, opposite the basilica. Farther off there was an old police jeep, possibly the only police car in town, and towards the river, one block beyond the plaza, you could see what looked like an open bar.

I stopped the car a few feet away from the girls and, without getting out, asked them, "That's a bar there, right?"

"What does it look like to you?" one of them, the darker one, replied, suddenly disappointed because there was a woman at my side.

"It looks like one to me, but I wanted to make sure. And is there a port here, or a dock? We need a boat."

The two of them started to laugh as though I had cracked a very good joke.

"It's still around two hours till dawn. Right now all the boatmen are sleeping."

"And besides, they say fishing's been bad lately," said the other one, who was a little fairer and chubbier.

"You can try in El Paso. It's near here."

"We need a boat," I said dryly. "And we need it here and right now. We were told there's fishing at dawn in this place we know about, and we're prepared to pay good money…"

Those turned out to be the magic words, of course. Their

mood changed; they paid attention; they became almost charm-ing. The dark one told us to wait with her friend while she went to look for Don Santos, who was her uncle and a good boatman and fisherman's guide. I told her if she wasn't back in ten minutes, we'd go right to the police for help and that we were paying good money for the services we required.

My blustering worked: the girl returned in exactly ten minutes, half dragging a man of indeterminate age, skinny and angular and wrinkled like a tortoise. Maybe he was only a couple of years older than I was, but he practically looked like my father. He had all the sunrises and sunsets of the Paraná on his skin, and he had endured hunger many times, mitigated only by fish. He might have been a good drinker, too. His eyes were full of veins, and his nose was quite veined, as well. I didn't like the guy at all, but there wasn't much choice on that early morning.

I got out of the car and we shook hands, and, as is the custom in Corrientes, I spoke first:

"Are you Don Santos?"

"At your service, *patrón.*"

"Very good. I'm Doctor Carlos Romero Taboada," I said ceremoniously, using a fittingly illustrious surname of that area.

"I'm listening, *patrón.*" The guy didn't seem overly im-pressed.

"We're not interested in fishing. The lady here has a fam-ily emergency. We've just been notified by phone, and we have to cross right away."

"Hmmm...." he said, giving me a typical Corrientes re-ply: he didn't believe me, but he didn't want to offend me, and besides, he needed to gain time while he thought about the risks he'd have to take and how much he would charge us for it. I could hear the noises in his brain: the gears were primitive but full of astuteness. What that man lacked in intelligence, he made up in craftiness.

"And where d'ya wanna go, eh, *patrón?*"

"To the other side. Nice and quick, no questions asked. Name a price."

"Ummm…" the wretch went on in his elusive style. He weighed our urgency so as not to err in the amount. I saw Griselda becoming apparently nervous, maybe overacting. But it helped.

Nevertheless, the guy preferred to pass the ball to my court.

"You decide, okay?"

"Five hundred pesos."

"Hmm…Thas' not even half," he said, looking at the ground. He couldn't look me in the eyes because he knew he was ripping me off.

"All right, let's suppose you say eight hundred and I accept. Deal?"

His eyes shone as he nodded his head. That bastard didn't earn eight hundred pesos in a whole month.

"How long will it take you to get the boat ready?" Griselda asked in an enormously annoyed voice. I realized she wasn't faking.

"Right away, *patrona,*" the guy said. "I always have it ready, so we'll be on our way. But s'gonna be rough, I'm warnin' ya."

"You two, come with us," I said to the girls, who were watching the scene like privileged witnesses, as though someone had given them box seats at the Circo Panamericano. "I'm going to pay you for another service, too."

I grabbed the suitcase and the bag of clothing, and I locked the car, wondering why I was doing it. And the five of us went towards the river, a few blocks farther down.

twelve

Of course the only thing I wanted was to keep them on the hook. The monkey dances for money, and the last thing we needed was for those girls to go blab to the entire town about our pre-dawn visit.

When we reached the coast, and the skinny man pushed an old wooden boat towards the water, I asked myself if we'd be able to cross the Paraná in that. It was a big, wide boat, about eighteen feet long, paunchy in the middle and all faded. In the stern, it held a little motor that looked like it came from a motorcycle. I was afraid because, aside from that, the river looked very choppy that morning. Griselda looked at me with fury – and panic – in her eyes, but both of us understood immediately that we had no other choice.

When the moment came to climb into the canoe, I gave a couple of fifty pesos bills to each of the girls.

"So that you'll forget about us at least until daylight," I recommended. The two of them smiled gratefully, saying of course and wishing us good luck and a safe trip.

I knew in any event it was quite possible that as soon as we left, both of them would go running to wake everyone up. But maybe not. They were intrigued by us, but they didn't seem like blabbermouths. I consulted Griselda with a glance. She gave me a wink to calm me down. Just the same, we had no choice.

What didn't calm anybody down was the river. I don't know if you're familiar with that fucking river, how it behaves: it's a blanket of silken water when it's calm, and there's no other calm quite like it. But when it's choppy, it's a wild sea. The Paraná is a living river – I mean, it has internal currents, fury, a mythology. I guess that's why those of us who know it consider it a fabulous river, admirable and hateful at the same time. You should see the fascination it holds for fishermen, and the respect swimmers have for it. No one takes chances; no one crosses it without having someone else beside him in a safe boat, for example. It's a river with a soul, you might say, and that night its soul was tormented. It was in a frenzy, and our fragile little boat (fragile as far as I was concerned) moved around like those small branches in the mouths of drainage ditches, turning and turning but never going down the drain until at last they're swallowed by the sewer.

Griselda was sitting in the middle of the canoe, on top of a board that went from one side to the other, clutching the oarlocks. She was perfectly aware of the danger, and she faced it with admirable fortitude. The wind disheveled her hair, the water plastered her dress to her skin, and she surely must have been very cold, but she didn't move except to accompany the swaying of the boat, and she didn't utter a single word. I rode in front, squatting, squeezed in some three feet from the prow, also clutching the sides. I had swung the bag with the clothing and the cops' pistols and bullets over my shoulder, and I pressed the briefcase tightly between my legs. Don Santos rode in back, sitting on a sort of little bench, attending to the gentle, monotonous noise of the little motor's pistons, which emitted a slightly weary, but constant, putt-putt-putt.

It was apparent that Don Santos was familiar with that frenzy and had confidence in his motor and in his boat. I knew that if he had figured we couldn't cross, he would have told us so. But the only thing he had warned us about was that it was going to be rough, not that it would be impossible. Skillfully, and I would say almost lovingly, the man steered the little boat into the wind for a while; immediately after, he guided it crossways, then straightened it out again, and so on. The river threw water on us from all four sides, and some of the waves seemed to cover us. I feared for our own safety, but also for the briefcase's: we hadn't taken the precaution of wrapping the bills in a plastic bag. Besides, you couldn't see a thing: we were sailing almost blindly, and we had no lights, just a little flashlight in the stern that Don Santos had turned off when he untied the canoe. I watched him more closely than I watched the river, attentive to his movements in spite of the darkness. The guy appeared to be calm, silent, and concentrating. I realized that he had to know exactly where we were: *baqueanos*[3] never get lost. They see in the shadows, like bats, and they might be dragged by a strong current or tossed about by a north wind, but they never lose the internal compass they've developed during so many years of floating and floating.

---

[3] *baqueano*: traditional pathfinder; guide.

There was one moment when I really felt afraid: when I noticed that no light was visible behind us. Itatí had disappeared, and there was no horizon or signpost in the world other than the depths of night. Barely a tenuous line, darker than darkness, perhaps imaginary, which one might suppose was the opposite shore. The river must be around two miles wide there, and although it wasn't raining, the overcast sky plunged us into a kind of humid, sticky vault with a watery base. But I also told myself it was an old fear, stemming from the time when I was a guy with lots of things to care for, when I had a lot to hold on to: in other words, a million years ago. Because at that moment, truly, the only thing I feared losing was my life, and maybe Griselda. I was so trivial, what I owned was so insignificant, that I told myself it was all right; if a lurch of the boat sent us straight to hell and everything ended, it was all right. Of course, I preferred not to die yet, and I was going to do everything within my power not to give up. Everything. That thought calmed me.

But then the little boat stopped abruptly, as if a superior hand had halted it. There was a sharp noise, like something sawing away beneath us, and the little motor sputtered, then fizzled out without warning. I realized we were grounded on a sandbar, surely exactly halfway across the river.

Swearing angrily, I asked the old man how it was possible, because it was inconceivable that a *baqueano* like him wouldn't know that the sandbar was there, even if that very afternoon it hadn't been visible and the river had just formed it. He answered me with the obvious: that he had calculated badly, that the current was stronger than he thought. He even said that we should already be in Paraguayan waters and that maybe someone from the Paraguayan Coast Guard would rescue us. Having said this, he jumped out of the canoe and tested the sand. The water didn't even reach his knees.

I realized right away that the guy was playing dumb. On

the one hand, he underestimated us, and on the other, he was trying to avoid crossing. The reason wasn't clear to me: maybe he had unfinished business with the Paraguayan authorities; maybe he had made an agreement with the girls and this was his way of turning us in to the Argentine Naval Prefecture. Yes, there was also the possibility that all of it was true: his silence and the possible appearance of a Paraguayan ship. But it was much more likely that the dude was faking. I decided that it didn't matter if I understood: the guy was shitting on us, so I didn't hesitate. I stepped over Griselda and stood in front of the guy, pointing the .38 in his direction.

"Are we going to cross, yes or no? Because that was the deal, understand?"

And with those words I put a bullet in his left leg, right at the level where the water reached it, beneath his knee. There was a muffled click, and the guy jumped and started shouting how could I do that to him, was I crazy, and he grabbed his leg and fell into the water and got up again. For a moment, I feared the current would sweep him away, but he was very adept: with one hand, he grabbed his wounded leg and with the other he held on to the edge of the boat. He climbed in, lying down beside the little boat. A lot of blood was flowing from that wound.

"Now listen to me, you son-of-a-bitch," I told him in a calm, but firm voice. "You have two alternatives: one, you make yourself a tourniquet, set this thing afloat again and take us to the Paraguayan coast nice and quick like we agreed and then go home and lick your wounds; or two, I'll plug you again and the piranhas or whatever the hell you call the fish in this fucking river can have you for lunch. Your choice."

The guy tied a rope around his leg at knee level and rapidly, silently, stuck an oar into the water, freeing the canoe. He started up the little motor by pulling a cord, and I swear to you, that feeble little boat seemed like it was flying. We reached the opposite shore in a few minutes. Without my having to ask him or give him an order, the guy headed for a sort of perfectly hidden natural harbor, typical of small-time smugglers, and told me that if we continued up the coast for about 500 feet, we'd find a path, like a narrow trail in the jungle, that would open up into a dirt road which in turn would lead to the nearest town, Desmochados.

I realized that the guy was really worried now. He kept touching his leg, as if to verify how much it ached him. I considered killing him but thought it would be excessive. It would cost me nothing to plug another bullet into him, and I confess I felt half tempted, but I decided to let him go. Whatever he might say when he got back would neither help nor hinder our situation. So I put the weapon down. And at that very moment Griselda took it from my hand and blew his head off.

thirteen

As we walked along the edge of the river, sometimes sinking into the muddy shore, conquering our fear of stumbling into some treacherous sinkhole that might plunge us into the quicksand, or into some nest of alligators, or whatever, I thought about how Don Santos had spun around like a marionette before he fell into the water to be carried off by the current, and about how that woman beside me was absolutely extraordinary in every way. She truly was capable of anything. Much more capable than I, or than anyone else I had ever met.

Suddenly she made me feel both fascinated and terrified.

I also thought about how tired I was and how it was time to call Eleuterio. I had complete faith in that phone call. In El Chaco, everyone understands what Paraguay means to fugitives. If you have a friend and some dough, you can get out of any kind of fix. I had both, and very few needs: a car and some Paraguayan papers in order to cross into Brazil. For Eleuterio, that was no big deal.

When we reached the path that Don Santos had indicated, it was already five thirty in the morning. Although it was an unlikely hour, the emergency of the situation and my anxiety ignored the time. I took the phone out of the bag, turned it to "roaming," and dialed his number. His answering machine picked up. I felt enormous relief when I heard his voice. Briefly, I reminded him of who I was and told him I was in very serious trouble, that I needed help urgently and would he please call me back on my cell phone, whose number I repeated twice. And I told him that in any event, I'd call back later that morning.

Then, as I was overcome with fatigue and didn't know what else to do, I suggested to Griselda that we sleep for a while, Indian-style, leaning against a tree.

"You sleep," was all she replied, lighting another cigarette.

I leaned the suitcase up against a beautiful *lapacho* tree, placing my bag of clothing on top of it. I leaned my head against it, conking out in less than a minute. I didn't dream at all. I had no strength for remorse or for fantasies.

When Griselda woke me, it was already dawn.

"The telephone's ringing," she informed me.

Half asleep and half anxious, I clumsily pressed the "on" button.

"Eleuterio here," he said. "Where are you and what's going on, buddy?"

I concisely told him that I was on a mountain near the river and near Desmochados, that I wasn't alone, and that I needed a safe place and maybe some papers and a car to cross over into Brazil.

"Are the pigs after you?"

"Yeah."

"Do you need money? Is it a business thing?"

"I don't need any money. Let's just say I went crazy over a skirt and I have to take a long trip. There's plenty of blood involved."

"Shit, Romerito, who would've guessed it?" he said ironically. "Okay, let me see what I can do for you. You sure you don't need money? Everyone needs money."

"No, I've got money."

"All right. Where are you, exactly?"

"No fucking idea. Near the coast, around Itatí, on a smugglers' path, I suppose."

"All right, give me a while to see what I can work out for you. Stay where you are, and we'll talk in half an hour."

He hung up.

I asked Griselda for a cigarette. She replied that there were none left.

"But we bought three packs last night."

"So?"

I preferred not to continue the argument I felt coming. I understood she was in a horrible mood. I wondered if on top of everything else she was about to get her period. Women go nuts when it's that time of the month. The day before their periods start, they're capable of committing murder. But I also knew that if I asked her, it would cost me dearly.

"Were you able to sleep a little?" I asked, just to say something.

She shook her head no, and I realized that she was tremendously upset. I don't know if it was fear, guilt, remorse, or what, but you could tell from a mile away that she was as screwed-up as a machine with all its gears in reverse.

I sat there gazing at the thicket. I wondered about the potential dangers: the appearance of animals or the presence of human beings. You couldn't hear anything but the noise of the birds and branches. It was terribly hot, but at least we were in the shade.

The phone rang again.

"Romero, can you hear me?" It was Eleuterio.

"Perfectly."

"You have to get to the road leading to Desmochados. You'll see a Coca Cola sign about a mile before. A couple of friends will pick you up there and take you to Ponce's place. Ponce, remember. Don't talk about anything to anyone; only to him. Ask him for whatever you need, and we'll never owe each other anything again, okay?"

"All right."

"And I never helped you and neither did anyone else, agreed? You got yourself in deep shit, Romero. Real deep."

"All right. Thanks a lot."

"There's no thanks necessary for this sort of thing. I'm paying back some favors and that's all. Good luck."

He hung up again.

fourteen

Less than an hour later, two guys in a brand new Isuzu 4x4 station wagon picked us up. They looked like brothers, or cousins: both young, thin, with mustaches, jeans, and boots. They looked like rich cowboys from the region, or something like that. They spotted us, braked the station wagon, opened up the rear doors and pulled away again, all in silence. In fifteen minutes we arrived in town.

They told us we could take advantage of the opportunity to go to the bathroom and wash up a bit, and they asked us if we wanted some *mate* [4] or coffee. Griselda asked for coffee and cigarettes and smoked two in a row. I took them up on the offer of *mate*, and they brought me a thermos, a *porongo* made of cow horn and filled with *yerba*, and a Brazilian *bombilla*, one of those big ones all decorated with gilt and fake rubies.

They left us alone in what seemed to be the living room of a house. There was a cheap sideboard, a living room set with vinyl upholstery, and on one wall, a frightful seascape representing a storm on a rocky coast that looked like the Norwegian fjords or something like that.

Griselda just smoked and sighed. I tried to speak to her calmly, reasonably, about our situation, but it was impossible: in short, I needed for us to be a team again. But there was no way: she had closed up like a clam. She looked at me resentfully, as though I had led her to that tenth circle of hell we seemed to be creating. It infuriated me because I thought it was unfair on her part. A touch of tenderness, let's say, would have been good for both of us; even in grave situations like ours, a caress, a word of mutual support, an act of kindness, are welcome, I don't know, a little bit of whatever you want to call it.

But there was no way. And that made me feel alone and furious. For the first time, I clearly asked myself why I didn't just kill her once and for all. Did I love her, really? Did I still love her like two days ago, like last night, like even a few hours ago? Could love really vanish so quickly?

At noon they advised us that they would take us to Caazapá to see Señor Ponce. We went in the same station wagon, with the same silent guys. The trip took a couple of hours, during which time I didn't stop wondering why they hadn't asked us absolutely anything at all, not even our names. They didn't ask us for our weap-

---

[4] *mate, or yerba mate*: herbal tea popular in Argentina, Uruguay, and Paraguay. Typically drunk from a hollowed- out gourd, also called a *mate* or *porongo*, and sipped through a metal straw or *bombilla*.

ons, either, which they obviously knew we had. Not even for the money, which they also had to know about.

We arrived at the town, which is in a sort of small valley which can be reached by crossing a river. We parked next to a modest-looking house, nothing ostentatious. They made us go into a study and motioned for us to wait there. Immediately a horrifying dwarf entered.

He was less than three feet tall and he was quite muscular, with open, but solid little arms, doll-like hands, short little fingers. His head was completely shaved, and his face was angular, with protuberant eyes and thick lips. He reminded me of those devils that they usually put in the apses of Gothic churches in Europe. But the most impressive thing of all was his neck, as thick as a leg, which appeared to join his head to his short little body with a wooden peg, or something like that. I was shocked when I saw him, but I observed something else in Griselda's eyes: repugnance. I thought what I've always thought: that it's pity to be a dwarf because dwarves are evil, resentful. It's a pity, a fuck-up by God to be born a dwarf. People shit on you your whole life long. And you shit on other people your whole life long by your mere presence. All dwarves are living rancor made flesh.

He hopped into one of the armchairs and looked at us, smiling, like a medieval gnome or as you might imagine medieval gnomes looked.

"Don Eleuterio asked me to help you," he began in a screechy voice that had a somewhat metallic quality, as though instead of passing through a throat, the guy's air passed through lead pipes, "and I'll be glad to do it. Just tell me exactly what it is you need."

"Why don't you tell us first who you are?" Griselda spat out aggressively. I would have preferred a different approach, but she beat me to it.

"Ponce," the dwarf said, his smile freezing. "I have no

other name but Ponce. And the lady's name is...?"

"Let's say the lady's name is Laura Romero and that she's a little bit tired," I intervened. "I hope you'll forgive her, Señor Ponce, and that you'll understand, too, that this is a real emergency. We need a car, passports, and help getting into Brazil."

"We have Paraguayan passports all arranged, Señor..."

"Romero. As I told you."

"We also have a mule, practically right outside the door."

I understood what he meant: in Paraguay, stolen cars with false papers are called mules. They can circulate freely throughout the country because generally those stolen automobiles are protected by the police itself.

"But a mule will only help us in Paraguay, Señor Ponce..."

"Naturally. Don Eleuterio told me to help you reach the border."

"I understand," I said, just to say something.

"In other words, you'll get rid of us there and maybe even turn us in," Griselda interrupted. Her cold gray eyes now were two red flames, full of little veins. She was furious, anxious, out of control. I was afraid she'd do something stupid. And she was about to.

"Perhaps some friends of mine in Ciudad del Este might help get you across to Foz, but that would cost you."

"How much?" Griselda asked, popping a cigarette into her mouth and looking for the lighter in her purse.

"Let's say half of whatever's in that suitcase Señor Romero is guarding so carefully."

"I knew you were going to blackmail us, you son-of-a-bitch," Griselda said coldly, pulling out not the lighter, but rather the .38 with the silencer. She pointed it at his forehead, and the shot splattered the back wall with something blackish that had been the dwarf's blood and brains.

"She's crazy," was all I could manage to think, but not say, as I picked up the suitcase and the bag and we exited the study and climbed into a gray 405 that was outside the door. The silent guys in the Isuzu had disappeared as though the siesta heat had made them evaporate.

fifteen

That escape was insanity, but at that point nothing could be sane or reasonable. I charged along the road to Ciudad del Este. All I knew was that we had to get to that city, the South American symbol and capital of all evil: there is no crime, vice, trap, drug, or hideout that can't be obtained in Ciudad del Este. The triple border that links three corrupt countries together has witnessed the birth and development of that city, engendered in the days of the dictator Alfredo Stroessner and bearing that same ominous name for years. At the close of the millennium, it's the place in South America, and perhaps in the entire world, with the fastest growth rate for everything: population, lousy quality of life, delinquency of every stripe.

I was sure that in such a place and with two hundred thousand dollars, it wouldn't be impossible for me to cross into Brazil.

Yes, of course, I said "for me" instead of "for us." That trip served to perfect my betrayal of Griselda. In spite of my fatigue, I didn't stop thinking about it for one second. I had her there at my side, and, naturally, she just smoked and looked at the landscape with an air of apparent indifference. We didn't speak to each other; it wasn't necessary. There was no comment we could share, no questions we could ask one another. Either of us could have any reaction to anything at all, and the other one would just accompany him in his escape.

Suddenly, I don't know why, I recalled several guys I had met who also had run away. I thought about what running away meant: once a guy had told me what running away meant to guerrillas, those who called themselves militant revolutionaries in those days. Of course, he said they weren't assassins or delinquents, but all of them carried their cross, and escape seemed to be their unavoidable destiny.

I also recalled the number of fugitives who had thrown themselves off General Belgrano Bridge since it was constructed. People said it had the highest number of suicides. They left their cars, bikes, and letters behind, and threw themselves into the river. I also remembered Norberto, a dear, childhood friend, who, when I was in exile in Misiones, committed suicide in Asunción, specifically in a crummy little fourth-rate hotel, poor, in debt, a human wreck. He was only thirty-eight, but he had an extraordinary sense of defeat that must have weighed on him like several tons of years. All his business ventures had gone sour on him, and he had gotten into debt with the banks and with several loan sharks. No one ever found out how much he owed, but one day he just disappeared. He left several children, a bitter widow, a frightful drama. And then he shot himself in Asunción. I've always had the feeling, silly of course, that maybe I could have done something. Or rather, the feeling that the tragedy of someone who had been my friend ended up being totally alien and distant from me. A shitty feeling.

And I also thought about Cacho Costacurta, who got into a brawl in a casino and finally took off, leaving a big mess behind. As it was assumed his business was going well – he owned a dairy wholesale outlet – several loan sharks gave him credit. And Cacho did it right: he disappeared one morning after having collected about a million in cash. He disappeared, causing a couple of heart attacks among well-known loan sharks in El Chaco, which earned him enormous popularity overnight. For several years, no one heard a word about him, and he was remembered as a mythical righter of wrongs who had pissed off a number of moneylenders. These, in turn, looked for him at first, in order to kill him, it was said, because Cacho had pulled things off very well. They couldn't foreclose on any of his mortgages because it turned out that nothing belonged to him: in effect, he had shit on everybody. But nevertheless, twelve years later, Cacho returned, and today he strolls around Resistencia, as smug as you please. You can usually find him at the Nino, at the old Estrella Bar. Now he works with young girls: he's always going around with some little whore at his side, one of those fourteen or fifteen-year-old kids who prostitute themselves in Resistencia and who swarm – a perfect symbol of Peyton Place – a few blocks around City Hall and the cathedral. He loves to shock the townspeople, Costacurta does. The fact is, these days no one bothers him; he has a humble kiosk attended by his mother and an aunt, and apparently he paid off his old debts or managed to get a pardon.

For my part, I never thought it would be exciting to be a

fugitive, but now everyone is after us: the good, the bad, and the worse, natives and foreigners. And I've got the bad luck to have a disturbed, cracked, completely unpredictable woman with me. Griselda had already done too many stupid things. I was fed up with her explosive temper. Besides, I foresaw that I'd have more possibilities of escaping, really, if I were alone. I needed to kill her; it was apparent that with her, it would be impossible to run away. I began to understand that I'd finally have to betray her. I didn't like the idea, but I couldn't see any other option. It made me feel guilty, I felt bad, but, no – I couldn't see any other option. Besides, something had broken. Love, well, at that moment, who could say what it was? It's impressive how love can evaporate in a few hours.

At my side, silently, Griselda was plunged into who-could-tell what kind of thoughts. She was smoking, and she didn't speak to me. She must have been depleted, exhausted, but she didn't sleep; she never slept. That incredible woman was immoderate in everything and as unpredictable as a she-cat, besides. She had nothing in common with the Griselda I had loved, that passionate, middle-class lady from Peyton Place. This one seemed inexhaustible; she *was* inexhaustible. In sex, in love, and in resentment, Griselda was like a fire that's never consumed. An eternal flame.

I had no choice but to extinguish it.

sixteen

Don't believe, of course, that I wasn't perfectly aware she must have been thinking exactly the same thing. On the back seat was a suitcase with two hundred thousand dollars in it, a .38 that had been very busy lately, and two slightly old, perhaps badly oiled, but nonetheless lethal .45's.

Suddenly I told myself it was a question of seeing who would strike first. In that business, I was going to be the quicker hand, although not necessarily the most astute.

And now I must also say something that – well, I don't

know if all this will seem too disgusting, repulsive, or perverted to you. I can imagine what you must be thinking. But, you know what? I don't care how you judge this tale. If you're still there, listening, and if you've gotten this far, just understand that this is my story and I can't tell it any other way than as it happened to me. I don't want to, either, because any moralizing would be superfluous, any ethical judgment would be too much at this moment. My life depends on what I'm telling you. Literally.

Because it all came down to the fact that one of us had to kill the other. We had reached a dead-end street, and just as I comprehended it, so did Griselda: either I killed her, or she was going to kill me. It wasn't even a question of determining if it was true we had stopped loving each other: no, what for? Why not admit that if love so often included crime, it could also include death? I think we still loved each other, and perhaps in the most total, absolute way, but now it was an incandescent love, you might say. A love that knows only how to burn. There are loves like that, in case you didn't know it; just as there are cold, contemplative loves, there are fiery loves. That's all they are: flames, conflagrations, burning coals, embers. They burn like the devil, and you go so insane that you want only to extinguish them.

Poor Griselda and I – we were at the same crossroads. Only the elimination of one of us would allow the other to survive. We had loved each other so much that we had lost our sense of limits. Neither one was guiltier than the other, neither one was salvageable, neither one better or worse. The terrible thing was to be so equal, such twins in our passion and in our insanity. Rancor and desperation, I then understood, have no sex; they lack genitalia. The lead you to commit the most heinous acts; they plunge you into an indescribable tenth circle of hell.

Around eight miles before reaching Ciudad del Este, I decided I had no choice but to kill her. I stopped the car gently on a curve of the highway, and saying I was too tired to go on, I opened the door and got out. Griselda remained seated, rigid, like an alert statue. I turned to open the back door, pretending I was looking for something in the bag. I planned to pull out one of the .45's and blow her to bits. But she beat me to it: when I took the pistol out of the bag and raised my eyes, she was aiming at me with the well-worn .45. I manage to avoid being shot in the face, but when I stood up, she hit me in the chest, and the impact threw me onto the shoulder. Then she got behind the wheel and threw it in reverse, driving over me a couple of times to finish me off. She was still looking out the window, and she fired another shot at me before skidding down the road.

She beat me to it. Some people might think that women always win. But it wasn't a question of sex; we were both bad, that's all, and we were desperate.

epilogue

But her mistake was to leave me for dead when I wasn't. I've already told you that when it comes to dying, some people are very tough. And evidently I'm one of them.

I've been in a coma, that's evident, too, and I don't know for how long or where. At this moment, I feel like I'm all bandaged up; I can hardly move, and this place smells like a hospital. I can smell the tea they're giving me to drink with a spoon and also the starched sheets, which are probably white. I've just awakened, like from a long dream, and I still haven't opened my eyes, but I'm already thinking about Griselda and if she knows I didn't die. Did she finally manage to escape? Could she be in Foz or in São Paulo, for example? Maybe in Rio or in Bahía, which was her dream.

Well, I'll look for her. Now I'm all bandaged up, with multiple wounds and a couple of bullets; I don't know if they've taken them out of me or if I'll always keep them inside my body, but I'm going to look for her and find her. She really fucked me up, the miserable bitch, but I belong to the category of tough guys, it's obvious. We're not easy to kill. It makes me feel good to feel this way.

I'm alive. The important thing is I'm alive. I don't know where or under what conditions, but I feel I'm alive. I'm breathing. She didn't kill me; the bitch couldn't kill me. She took the dough, but she couldn't kill me.

And I'm going to look for her, naturally, and I'm going to find her. Somewhere I'll find her.

Even though there might be a cop outside this room, as there should be. Even if there's a trial and they convict me, as they surely will. Some day I'll get out and I'm going to find her. For sure.

I've barely opened my eyes, and it fascinates me to see the light. It's a re-encounter with life, with movement, although the only movement here comes from this nurse who's spooning tea into my mouth. It does me good. Lots of good. I'll drink lots of tea, and I'll recover and then I'll go look for her.

Oh, Griselda, my darling Griselda, when I find you…

Because sooner or later I'm going to recuperate. I don't know how I'm going to kill you, Griselda, but I swear I'll do it. I can't come up with schemes yet, but I'm going to find you and I'm going to kill you. I know I still love you, but at the same time, you're what I hate most. I hate you more than anything else in the world. And I won't stop until I blow you away.

The nice, warm tea does me good. It flows through my

insides and creates a pleasant, sweet sensation in me. I open my eyes to give thanks for it, just as I give thanks for the light I can see once again. Light, what a marvelous thing! Nice and slowly, calmly, and even though it blinds me a little, I can see again...It's fantastic. The nurse smiles at me; she has a lovely smile beneath her nurse's cap. I close my eyes, thinking of that pretty smile. Until it dawns on me, and I open my eyes, terrified, because I recognize that smile, beneath Griselda's gray eyes that regard me with the coldness of marble, of an iceberg.

"I'm sorry, my love, but twice is too much," she says.

It's the last thing I manage to hear before the final shot rings out.

Gijón. Andalusia. Lisbon. May/June 1998.